SPACE CHIMPS ™

THE SIMIAN SPACE MANUAL

By Rebecca McCarthy *and Ham III*

Based on the original screenplay by Kirk De Micco

PSS!
PRICE STERN SLOAN

Space Chimps TM & © 2008 Vanguard Animation, LLC. All Rights Reserved. Published by Price Stern Sloan,
a division of Penguin Young Readers Group, 345 Hudson Street, New York, New York 10014.
PSS! is a registered trademark of Penguin Group (USA) Inc. Printed in Mexico.

ISBN 978-0-8431-3227-4   10 9 8 7 6 5 4 3 2 1

As one of NASA's Space Chimps, you must prepare for the challenges of space exploration. You will be subjected to harsh conditions and dive headfirst into danger. You will be held to extremely high standards of excellence. You will lead your country into the future. You will be among the few, the proud, the Space Chimps.

HAM'S NOTES: This manual is a bunch of hogwash written by humans. It's only real use on a real space mission is to be torn up into confetti and thrown at scary snake monsters. But just in case you don't have a need for confetti on your mission, I've written in some tips and tricks that might actually be helpful. So ignore what those silly humans wrote and just focus on my words of wisdom! This is serious, so stop picking the lint out of your belly button, okay?

As a space chimp, you must be ready for anything. You will run three miles every morning with your fellow Space Chimps. Chanting together helps keep the pace steady. Here is an example of a good running chant:

I'm a space chimp, I am strong
I like running all day long!
Run so hard my muscles burst
We all know that chimps go first!
Sound off
One, two!
Once more
Three, four!
Bring it on down now
One, two, three, four
One, two, THREE, FOUR!

You will also be required to pass tests to make sure you are ready for space flight. You will be strapped into a machine that rotates at very fast speeds. Try to stay awake during these tests.

HAM'S NOTES:

Ham's revised running chant:

I'm a space chimp, I am strong
I can't stand this silly song!
Run so hard my muscles burst
Please don't sing another verse!
Sound off
Bor-ing!
One, two
To the core!
Bring it on down now
One, two, three, four
I don't want to sing ANYMORE!

As a space chimp, you are expected to be clean and neat at all times. This means no frayed collars or cuffs, no patches, and no holes in the knees of your uniform.

When in uniform you must stand at parade rest or at attention. To stand at parade rest, clasp your hands behind your back with feet shoulder-distance apart. To stand at attention, place your hands at your sides with feet together and chest held high.

After your heroic mission, the city might host a parade in your honor. For parades, you may wear your formal attire, which is the same uniform but with medals, ribbons, and impressive sparkly things on it.

HAM'S NOTES: Shades are also to be worn whenever an extra degree of coolness is necessary. For example, before a mission, you are to don your shades and walk across the tarmac to your spaceship in slow motion. Arrange to have music played in the background while you walk, for maximum effect.

UNIFORM DIAGRAM

HELMET LOCKING MECHANISM

HELMET

Racing stripes

Zippers that serve no purpose

OFFICIAL SPACE AGENCY PATCH

TETHER CORD PLUG

Useful for surfing through space behind your ship

STANDARD-ISSUE TOOL BELT

REFLECTIVE SPACE SUIT

Protects you from radiation and space dust, but NOT from evil alien dictators!

KNEE PADS

HAM'S NOTES:

Unless it's Titan. In which case you'd say, "Whatever, dude."

As a space chimp, you are expected to respect your fellow chimps. You should always treat elders with the utmost courtesy. It is important to address one another by your ranks and titles. Always use the proper language when making requests, asking questions, and giving orders. For example, to say "Yes" to your commanding officer, you would say, "Yes sir" or "Yes ma'am."

It's a good idea to add the word "chimp" into daily conversation to show your space chimp spirit. For example, instead of saying, "You're a chip off the old block," you would say, "You're a chimp off the old block." Other fine examples of chimp-speak include "Chimp-martial," "*Chimpfinity*," and "Chimp-tastic!" Do this often. Your crewmates will think you are clever and funny. No, no they will not.

6

The Simian Program uses the traditional military ranking system to classify its crew. The following is a list of ranks, in order from highest to lowest. Memorize these rankings and salute superior ranks at all times.

- Fleet Admiral
- Admiral
- Vice Admiral
- Rear Admiral (Upper Half)
- Rear Admiral (Lower Half)
- Captain
- Commander
- Lieutenant Commander
- Lieutenant
- Lieutenant Junior Grade
- Ensign

HAM'S NOTES:

Ham's alternative ranking system:

- Head Honcho
- The Grand Enchilada with Extra Cheese
- The Grand Enchilada
- Mr. Kind of a Bigger Deal
- Mr. Kind of a Big Deal
- Big shot
- Chump
- Drone
- Pawn
- Spam
- Human

There are rocket packs located in the small cargo bay at the rear of the bridge. They can be used to increase mobility on unfamiliar territory. Should you land your ship on a planet with steep mountains, deep craters, or even an all-liquid surface, the rocket packs should be used for safe travel. *Oh, so that's what those are for!*

In cases of extreme emergency, this ship is equipped with a twenty-four-hour automatic fail-safe system. Twenty-four hours after a crash landing, the ship will begin the liftoff sequence again and return home on autopilot. If you would like help before that time, there is an InStar button that employs the most comprehensive security, communications, and diagnostics system on the planet.

HAM'S NOTES: *Uh, helleeew? The nice InStar lady only speaks human. Wouldn't it be better to patch the ship in to a direct line with Comet, or some other computer-repair genius that speaks chimp? Helleeew?*

SHIP DIAGRAM

For watching meteor showers while you are taking a shower

PORTHOLES

HULL

RUDDER

WINGS

In a pinch, an alien dictator frozen in freznar can work

NOSE CONE

VIEWING DECK

PROPULSION SYSTEM

LAUNCH BOOSTERS

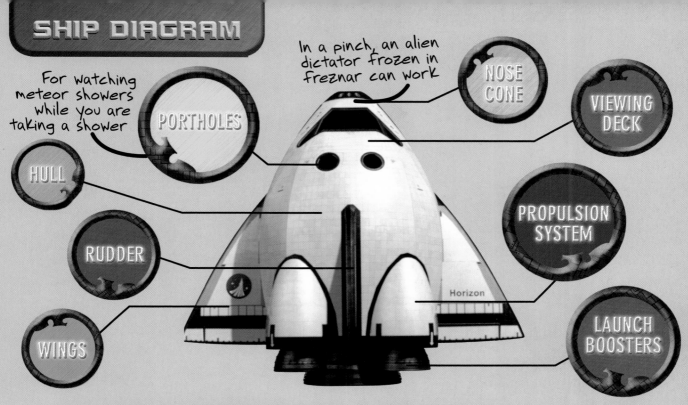

Horizon

How to Woo Your Fellow Female Crewmate

Dear Reader,

Some pages of your Simian Space Manual said some nonsense about how crewmembers aren't allowed to go out together on dates or fall in love. Well that's just silly! Going on a dangerous, life-threatening mission together is a perfect recipe for luuuuv!

If you are lucky enough to go up in space with an attractive crewmate, by all means, do everything you can to impress her. Do cartwheels and somersaults so she can see how athletic you are. When you enter a room, reach up and high-five the door frame (easier to do in zero gravity) so she can see how high you can jump. Make jokes at all times, even when she's trying to ask you a serious question, because girls like guys with a good sense of humor.

When it's time to introduce yourself, try one of these pickup lines:

- "Your eyes are as brown as dirty dishwater."
- "I love your coat. They say ginger's the new black."
- "I know a great little nebula where they make the best cannoli."

Most important of all, you've got to remember three little words: "You're right, dear." You don't want to get towed back to Earth from behind the ship!

To keep a commander's log, you must always start by stating the current star date. The star date includes the calendar date and your ship's location in the galaxy.

Use the standard regulation recording device on your wrist to make notes about your mission. Tip: You never know who is listening to your recordings back on Earth, so keep it professional.

HAM'S NOTES:

To calculate a star date, start with the calendar date. Say, for example, November 2, 2008, 1:30 P.M. Take the number of years since the last leap year and multiply it by the number of licks it takes to get to the center of a Tootsie Pop. Then multiply that by 100,000 and divide by the number of minutes you spend playing video games per week. Then add the number of hours that have passed already today, and then read it all out loud. The result should be something like, "Commander's Log. Star date 96839.5." . . . Or you can just say, "Thursday."

"Can you believe that tie he wore to the Christmas party last year? And, uh, repeat after me: A helmet. Is not. A fashion accessory. A helmet. Is not. A fashion accessory. And when did Vogue declare 'millennium silver' as the new black?"

11

HAM'S NOTES:

What does the "T" stand for? Terrified? Too scary? Take me off this crazy thing?

To remember this sequence, use one of Titan's dorky poems: "Take it from the liftoff master, first press red, then press green. If you want to get there faster, then press 2-5 in between."

Dumb, but I have to admit, it works.

To prepare for liftoff, all chimponauts should sit at their stations with safety belts fastened. The countdown will begin thus: T-minus ten, nine, eight, seven . . . etc.

To activate the ship's liftoff controls, punch the following sequence into the control panel: Red 2-5 Green.

Once the ship is in space, you should immediately engage the 3-D matrix and ready visual imaging. Check your orbital stabilizers, auxiliary thrusters, and other systems needed for landing.

HAM'S NOTES:

Please turn off all portable electronic devices, including laptops, iPods, and CD players, as they may interfere with the communication system. Please remain seated until your captain turns off the "fasten seat belt" sign, at which point you may feel free to walk about the cabin. Thank you for choosing Chimpfinity Airlines, and we hope you have a pleasant flight.

How to lift off from a volcano:
1. Place ship onto volcano
2. Hold on for dear life
3. Wait for volcano to erupt
4. Scream for your mama

HAM'S NOTES:

Again, Titan's dorky poem will help you out with this one: "Fire the engines true and fast. Red one first. Blue one last. In between press 3-6-5, if you want to stay alive." Gotta hand it to the guy, it's catchy.

Riiiiiight. Those things sent us over the edge of a cliff!

First, review the landing activation sequence, which is Red 3-6-5 Blue.

Then align your thrusters for entry into the planet's atmosphere. If traveling through a wormhole or other such dimensional anomaly, secure a pillow behind your head because the g-forces will put you right to sleep. As you approach the planet's surface, release the landing gear. If the landing is bumpy, the air bags may deploy for your safety.

Ham's Tips for Landing Unsafely—
which is how it's usually done

1. First, make sure you're flying a real ship, where the controls are actually hooked up.

2. Activate the landing sequence.

3. When the landing sequence doesn't work, engage the ailerons, flick the turbulence coolers on, adjust the heat deflectors, and enable the gyroscopic stabilizers—all at once.

4. When the ailerons, turbulence coolers, heat deflectors, and gyroscopic stabilizers don't work, lower the landing gear.

5. When the landing gear doesn't work, prepare to steer the ship to a gentle, upright landing.

6. When the steering controls don't work, prepare to crash.

7. Keep your chin down, opposable thumbs in.

8. Try to hit something soft.

The hatch on your spaceship is sealed for your protection. If you land on a planet and see no immediate signs of danger, you may unlock and open the hatch.

To test for oxygen, open the hatch. If you can breathe, the air is good. If you suffocate from lack of oxygen in the planet's atmosphere, then that indicates a lack of oxygen in the planet's atmosphere. *Ummm . . .*

To test for gravity, open the hatch. If you stay on the ground, there is sufficient gravity for you to travel outside the ship safely. If you float away into outer space, never to be heard from again, there is not.

Should you encounter hostile alien creatures, you must be polite. You do not want to start an interplanetary war.

HAM'S NOTES:

Man, whoever wrote this book is a genius . . .

16

If you encounter peaceful alien creatures, by all means, attempt to befriend them. Start by introducing yourself and telling them about Earth. Tell them you mean them no harm, and would like to learn more about their planet.

Nah, that doesn't work. You gotta speak the universal language—dance! Put a big smile on your face and start poppin' and lockin', do the Bus Stop, do the Robot, King Tut, King Lear, Norman Lear, do the Bartman, Cabbage Patch, Ickey Shuffle . . .

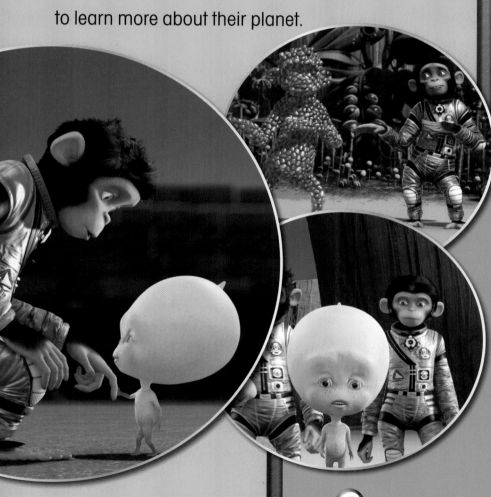

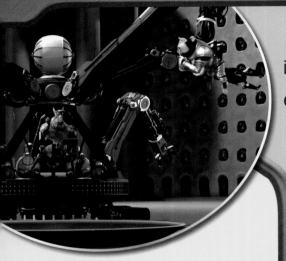

HAM'S NOTES:

"Hey—how about those Knicks? You think they'll go all the way this year? I love your home. Fabulous window treatments. PLEASE DON'T EAT ME!!!!"

To avoid capture by hostile aliens, run. However, if you are captured, follow these simple steps for escape:

1. **Talk to your captor. Find out what he wants, his likes, dislikes, and what he wants to do with you. See if there is any information you can use to your advantage.**

2. **If the alien says he plans to eat you for supper, stall for time. Try to change his mind.**

3. **Try to convince the alien that it is better for him to keep you alive. Offer to help him with a project. Offer to show him your spaceship.**

4. **Once you've gained his trust, he should let you walk about. When he does, RUN!**

Escaping capture is very complex. It's much easier to just run and not get captured in the first place. Perhaps you should start getting in shape. Who, me? Yes, you. Huh??

As stated earlier, we Earthlings have never encountered alien life, so this chapter will be largely speculative.

So, let's say an evil alien captures one of Earth's space provers and is using it to control other aliens. First, you should try to make a deal with him. Tell him you will show him how to use the "Universal Domination Sequence." Tell him to hit the yellow button, then turn the blue knob, then pull the lever, and then turn the green knob. This is actually the Ejection Sequence and the evil ruler will be thrown miles up into the air. Hopefully, he will land in a pool filled with petrifying liquid, which will turn him into a statue and thereby render him powerless.

HAM'S NOTES:

That means you have no idea what you're talking about and you're just guessing, right?

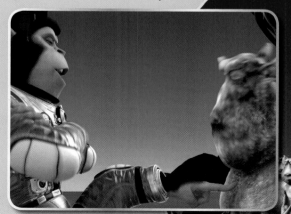

HAM'S NOTES:

No, really? I was gonna plan my next vacation there. Seriously, people— who wrote this stupid manual?!

NOT!!! One of those pretty flowers might actually be a twelve-headed snake in disguise! And the vines in the jungle might have sharp-toothed mouths on their ends!

Like Luna!

Since we have yet to encounter any kind of alien life, you probably do not need to worry about hostile creatures and rough terrains. However, there is a first time for everything, so it is best to be prepared. Here are some simple guidelines to follow when exploring new planets:

Pay attention to names. If a friendly alien tells you to beware of the "Deep Dark Cave of No Return," it is probably not safe to go there. Also steer clear of such places as "The Mountain of Evil," or "The Pond of Blood-Sucking Monsters."

If you encounter a planet with rich animal and plant life, feel free to take samples.

Creatures with warm fuzzy fur, large brown eyes, and cute tails are probably safe to approach. It would be wise to avoid creatures with claws and fangs.

. . . like Luna when she's mad.

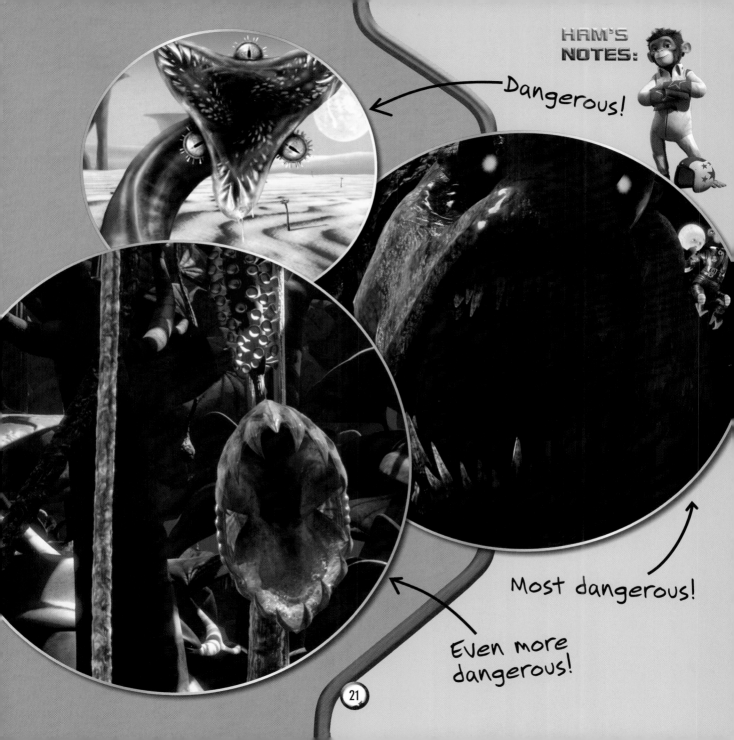

HAM'S NOTES:

LAME! Comet modified our walkie-talkies so we can communicate all the way back to Earth even from as far away as Malgor! This manual needs to be updated. I'm gonna write the Simian Space Manual Version 2.0! ... Later. When I get a chance. I'm kind of busy now, with my chimponaut career and all.

A space chimp never travels without certain items. These gadgets, trinkets, and tools are meant to be with you at all times.

1. The *Simian Space Manual*. When you need help in any difficult situation, consult your manual first.
2. Bananas. You must remember to stay well-fed and hydrated while in space.
3. A flashlight.
4. A helmet. For extra protection when using the rocket packs, or during turbulent space flight.
5. A wrist unit recording device. To record information on your journey and keep a log.
6. Walkie-talkies. These are for each of the crewmembers to communicate with one another should they have to separate while exploring a planet.

Hi, fellow Space Chimps! I'm Comet, the space chimp electronic specialist. Modifying and repairing computers and other electronic devices is really easy. Let's start with your walkie-talkies. The ones the Space Agency issues are kind of primitive, so it would be a good idea to modify them for use over greater distances—even wormholes. All you have to do is up-amp the heterodyne receivers, combine the micro-frequencies, and cross-switch the luminal signal.

Heh-heh. What the little guy is saying is, make the walkie part bigger, and the talkie part faster, and then cross this blue wire with this red thingy, and voilà! You have a BananaBerry!

If you hear static while communicating from space, just have mission control hack into the mainframe to filter the signal.

Or do it the old-fashioned way and just yell louder.

If communication becomes limited to one-way, then calibrate the Gregorian array, replace the helix mirror, and cross-feed the surrounding shroud.

In other words, if they can hear you but you can't hear them, just . . . call Comet and have him fix it.

If you need to rebuild an entire ship, or modify a space probe to be flown just like a spaceship, start by reengineering the skeletal structure. Then you'll need sixteen million mega-newtons of thrust.

Translation: Duct tape some new whooziwhatsits to the metal thing-um and go sit on a volcano.

THE CHIMP'S GUIDE
TO THE GALAXY

By Kate Ritchey
Based on the original screenplay by Kirk De Micco

PRICE STERN SLOAN

Published by Price Stern Sloan, a division of Penguin Young Readers Group,
345 Hudson Street, New York, New York 10014.
PSS! is a registered trademark of Penguin Group (USA) Inc. Printed in Mexico.

ISBN 978-0-8431-3227-4   10 9 8 7 6 5 4 3 2 1

The universe is a big place. One galaxy in the universe, called the Milky Way, has well over 200 billion stars in it. Our solar system is just one of many others in the galaxy.

A solar system is made up of a star and the space matter that travels around it. The Sun is the star at the center of Earth's solar system. Planets, moons, asteroids, and comets all move around the Sun in patterns called orbits.

The planets are the biggest things orbiting the Sun. There are eight planets: Mercury, Venus, Earth, Mars, Jupiter, Saturn, Uranus, and Neptune. The four planets closest to the Sun are made of rock, while the four farthest planets are made of gas and ice.

The objects in Earth's solar system are far away from one other. (The closest planet to Earth, Venus, is 23.7 million miles away!) But beyond the solar system, objects are so far apart that distances are measured in light-years instead of miles or kilometers. Light moves very quickly, at about 190,000 miles per second. A light-year is the distance light can travel in a full year, which is 5.9 trillion miles. The closest star to the Sun is about 4.2 light-years away—that's about 25 trillion miles!

HAM SAYS:

Except for Earth, the planets are named after Greek or Roman gods or goddesses. Many of the planets' moons are, too. I think they should be renamed after space heroes like me. They could be Ham 1, Ham 2, Ham 3 . . .

Mercury—Messenger god
Venus—Goddess of love
Mars—God of war
Jupiter—King of the gods

Saturn—God of agriculture
Uranus—God of the sky
Neptune—God of the sea

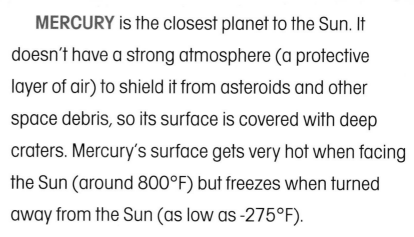

MERCURY is the closest planet to the Sun. It doesn't have a strong atmosphere (a protective layer of air) to shield it from asteroids and other space debris, so its surface is covered with deep craters. Mercury's surface gets very hot when facing the Sun (around 800°F) but freezes when turned away from the Sun (as low as -275°F).

Mercury is the smallest planet with the fastest orbit—it travels around the Sun in only 88 Earth days. But even though it moves through space quickly, it turns on its axis very slowly. One day on Mercury is equal to about 59 Earth days. That means that on Mercury, one year is only a day and a half long!

HAM SAYS:

Mercury is hard to see in the sky because it's so close to the Sun. But when it reaches the farthest point from the Sun in its orbit, it is visible from Earth just before dawn or just after sunset. Now that's worth getting up early to see!

○ ○ ○ ○

VENUS is the hottest planet in the solar system. Its atmosphere is full of carbon dioxide and sulfuric acid, which traps heat on the planet. The temperature there can reach up to 864°F!

Venus is about the same size as Earth. It is a very slow-moving planet: It orbits the Sun in about 225 Earth days, but turns on its axis in about 243 Earth days, so a day on Venus is longer than a year on Venus!

HAM SAYS:

Most of the places on the surface of Venus have been named for famous women and goddesses, such as Aphrodite, Sacajawea, Ishtar, Guinevere, and Niobe. Maybe they'll name the next place they find Luna.

EARTH is the third planet from the Sun and the only place in the universe known to have living things on it. Its distance from the Sun, amount of liquid water, and breathable atmosphere make life possible. Earth is about 93 million miles from the Sun. This distance, plus protection from the atmosphere, allows Earth's temperature to stay between -126°F and 136°F on the surface.

Earth has strong enough gravity that it has a satellite orbiting it. Earth's satellite is known as the Moon. The Moon is a large chunk of rock that travels around Earth once every 27.3 days. It's only about one quarter the size of Earth. Because of its size, the Moon affects the Earth: Wherever the Moon moves in the sky, it pulls Earth's water toward it, which creates the ocean tides.

HAM SAYS:
Earth's gravity slowed the Moon's rotation on its axis over many years. Now it is permanently stopped, so we can see only one side of the Moon from Earth. Let's hope it's the Moon's good side!

MARS is the small planet just beyond Earth. It is covered in red soil, giving it the nickname the Red Planet. It has huge volcanoes, including Olympus Mons, the largest volcano in the solar system, and dust storms that blow hard enough to cover the whole planet.

There is no breathable air on Mars. Scientists have found a lot of water just under the surface of the planet in the form of ice. They think that the cold, dry planet may once have been warm and wet, similar to Earth. They even think that life might have existed on Mars in its past!

HAM SAYS:
Mars has two satellites, Phobos and Deimos. In Greek mythology, Phobos and Deimos are the sons of Ares (whose Latin name is Mars).

Beyond Mercury, Venus, Earth, and Mars lies an asteroid belt, separating them from the largest planet in the whole solar system. **JUPITER** is a gigantic planet covered in bands of swirling gases. More than 1,300 Earths could fit inside it! It has at least 63 moons, the four biggest called Callisto, Europa, Ganymede, and Io. It has a single, barely visible ring traveling around it.

Despite Jupiter's size, it spins on its axis faster than any other planet: Its day is only about 10 hours long! This high speed causes intense winds which wrap the planet's clouds around it in bands. These bands are full of strong storm systems. One of these raging storms is called the Great Red Spot, and it's been swirling across Jupiter for more than 300 years.

HAM SAYS:
Jupiter spins very quickly on its axis—a day there is only about 10 hours long. But because it's very far from the Sun, a year there is more than 4,330 Earth days. And you thought your school year was long!

SATURN is probably the most recognizable planet because of the huge rings that orbit it. The rings are made of pieces of ice and rock that can be as small as a grain of sand or as big as a house! Saturn has thousands of rings, and they all move at different speeds around the planet. Saturn also has over 50 moons.

Saturn is the farthest planet from Earth known since ancient times. It's not as colorful as Jupiter because its lower temperatures turn chemicals in Saturn's atmosphere into ice crystals and create white clouds.

HAM SAYS:

One of Saturn's moons, Iapetus, has one white side and one black side. The light side is ten times brighter than the dark side, which scientists think has picked up dark space material during its orbit. Someone needs to take Iapetus in for a moon wash!

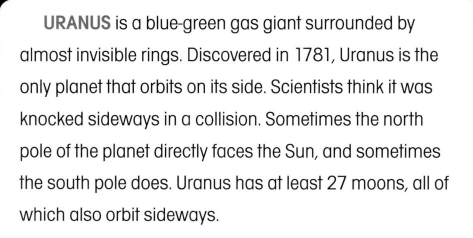

URANUS is a blue-green gas giant surrounded by almost invisible rings. Discovered in 1781, Uranus is the only planet that orbits on its side. Scientists think it was knocked sideways in a collision. Sometimes the north pole of the planet directly faces the Sun, and sometimes the south pole does. Uranus has at least 27 moons, all of which also orbit sideways.

Uranus has rings around it, but they are very dark, unlike Saturn's bright and colorful rings. Uranus is the farthest planet visible with the naked eye.

URANUS

NEPTUNE

NEPTUNE is the farthest planet from the Sun in the solar system. It is very similar to Uranus in size, but it looks bright blue instead of blue-green. Neptune was the last planet discovered in our solar system when it was spotted in 1846.

Like the other gas giants, Neptune has a system of rings encircling it. The rings are uneven, bigger on one side than the other. Neptune has six rings and at least thirteen satellites, including the moon Triton, and is the coldest place in the solar system. Neptune is also a very windy planet—the wind there gusts up to three times stronger than on Jupiter and nine times stronger than on Earth!

HAM SAYS:

In 2011, it will have been one Neptunian year since the discovery of the planet! A Neptunian year is almost 165 Earth years long. Go Neptune, it's your birthday! Get busy, it's your birthday!

OTHER OBJECTS IN SPACE

The eight planets are the largest things in the solar system (other than the Sun). But they aren't the only things traveling around in space!

ASTEROIDS are chunks of rock that travel through space in between the planets. They orbit the Sun the same way that the planets do, but they are very small and have weak gravity. Asteroids can be found throughout the solar system, but mainly they orbit in the Asteroid Belt, which is in between Mars and Jupiter.

KUIPER BELT OBJECTS (KBOs for short) are large icy boulders that resemble asteroids. They orbit in the Kuiper Belt beyond Neptune. Scientists believe that many comets originate there.

COMETS are chunks of ice, frozen gases, rock, and dust that speed through space toward the Sun from the outer edge of the solar system. The heat of the Sun warms up the comet as it gets closer and it begins to thaw, leaving gas and dust behind it. This trail of gas and dust looks like a bright tail from Earth. Comets travel toward the Sun, circle around it, and then head back out toward the edge of the solar system again.

HAM SAYS:

When pieces of space matter come through Earth's atmosphere and reach the surface, they are called meteorites. And they're pretty, but don't let one hit you in the head!

DWARF PLANETS

To be called a planet, a celestial body must:

1. orbit the Sun;
2. be large enough for gravity to crush it into a rounded shape;
3. clear other objects out of the area around its orbit.

There are some objects in space that are not quite planets but are not asteroids or comets, either.

A DWARF PLANET is an object that meets the first two requirements for a planet but not the third, and is also not a satellite. From 1930 until 2006, Pluto was considered a planet. But because it does not satisfy the third requirement, it is now a dwarf planet.

Pluto is a frozen land far out in the solar system. Its orbit crosses the orbit of Neptune, so that for twenty years in its 248-year orbit, it is closer to the Sun than Neptune is. Pluto is tiny—it's even smaller than Earth's Moon!

No spacecrafts have ever visited Pluto because it is so far away. But in January 2006, NASA launched the *New Horizons* craft to explore both Pluto and the Kuiper Belt. The spacecraft is expected to reach Pluto in July 2015.

THE SUN AND STARS

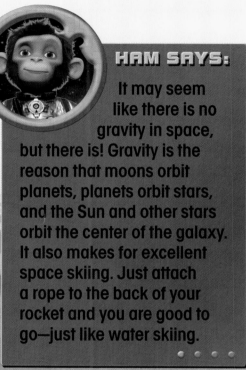

HAM SAYS:

It may seem like there is no gravity in space, but there is! Gravity is the reason that moons orbit planets, planets orbit stars, and the Sun and other stars orbit the center of the galaxy. It also makes for excellent space skiing. Just attach a rope to the back of your rocket and you are good to go—just like water skiing.

The Sun is the star at the center of the solar system. It is massive! It's 109 times bigger than Earth. The Sun is made mostly of hydrogen and helium. The core of the star burns at about 27,000,000°F. The Sun gives off all the heat and the light in the solar system.

There are six layers of the Sun: the core, the radiative zone, the convective zone, the photosphere, the chromosphere, and the corona. The first three layers are inside the Sun, the photosphere is the visible surface, and the chromosphere and the corona are the Sun's atmosphere. During a solar eclipse, the corona is all that is visible around the outside of the Moon's dark shape.

The Sun is only one of billions of stars. Some are bigger and others smaller than the Sun, but they are all balls of gas that create huge amounts of energy. All of the stars orbit around the center of a galaxy in the same way that planets orbit around a star. The closest star to the Sun is named Proxima Centauri, and it is 4.2 light-years away. The brightest star visible from Earth is called Sirius A, and it is 8.6 light-years away.

There are many different types of stars. They come in different sizes, different temperatures, and even different colors! Red stars are the coolest (around 3,800–5,800°F) and blue stars are the hottest (from 52,000–72,000°F). The biggest stars are called hypergiants and supergiants.

GALAXIES

Every star visible from Earth is part of the Milky Way Galaxy. There are well over 200 billion stars in the Milky Way! Galaxies are groups of stars and their solar systems. The Milky Way is shaped like a giant disk with a bump in the center where a large number of star systems are.

The Sun is about 25,000 light-years from the center of the galaxy. From Earth, the other stars in the Milky Way appear to cluster in a line, looking like a hazy band of light across the night sky. (It's easiest to see this band from June to September.) But the stars are spread out over the whole galaxy, about 100,000 light-years wide and 2,000 to 10,000 light-years deep.

HAM SAYS:

Astronomer Edwin Hubble classified galaxies into four shapes: spirals, barred spirals, ellipticals, and irregulars. The Milky Way is a spiral galaxy. I'd like to find a banana-shaped galaxy!

Although most other galaxies are too far away to see from Earth, a few are visible. The Andromeda Galaxy, discovered by Edwin Hubble, lies right between the constellations Cassiopeia and Pegasus in the night sky. It's a larger spiral galaxy than the Milky Way and has two smaller galaxies orbiting around it. Andromeda is 2.4 million light-years away, making it the farthest object the naked eye can see.

The Magellanic Clouds, two small, irregular galaxies, are visible from Earth's southern hemisphere. The larger galaxy is about 160,000 light-years from the Milky Way and about 30,000 light-years wide. Both galaxies are satellite galaxies of the Milky Way.

BLACK HOLES

If moons orbit around planets and planets orbit around stars, what do stars orbit around? Scientists think they may orbit around black holes.

A black hole is formed when the core of a gigantic star collapses. It shrinks, and gravity squashes the matter in the star. The gravity becomes so strong and powerful that light cannot escape from it. Since objects must be lit to be visible, the star disappears, leaving a black hole.

It's hard for scientists to learn much about black holes. Even if we were able to travel to one (The closest one is thought to be 1,600 light-years away!), we couldn't get very close to it. If a ship got too close to a black hole, it would get sucked in by the hole's gravity and it wouldn't be able to escape or transmit information back to Earth, because even radio waves could not escape the gravity.

HAM SAYS:

Wormholes are one answer to what might happen if you traveled through a black hole. You might enter the black hole and get sucked through a wormhole into another time or another galaxy. This is fun to imagine, but human scientists say that this couldn't really happen. We chimps know better, though.

ALIENS?

Could there be life somewhere else out in the universe? Right now Earth is the only place we know of that can support life. But the universe is a big place, and it is possible that there is life somewhere else. Scientists look for signs that life could exist on every new planet they explore and in every new galaxy they discover. They send out deep space probes and include written messages and records with sounds from Earth on them in case an intelligent being finds them.

But it isn't just scientists who wonder about life on other planets. People love to think about what it would be like if we met creatures from another world! Would they be small and green and have antennae? Would they be tall and fluffy and have seven arms? Would we be able to communicate with them somehow? Would they be friendly, or would they be cruel? Are they out there looking for us?

Humans are very interested in the idea that we are not alone in the universe. We would like to find others like us whom we can communicate with about our experiences. We want to learn more about the world we live in, how it started, and how it works. Maybe one day we'll discover life somewhere else as we continue to travel and explore in space.

HUMANS IN SPACE . . . .

People have stared at the stars for thousands of years and wondered what is out there. Ancient civilizations tracked the patterns of the sky to discover planets and stars, and then instruments like telescopes were invented to study space more closely. In the 1950s and 1960s, people became determined to travel into space.

Once they began, the first steps into space happened very quickly. The first artificial satellite, *Sputnik 1,* was launched into space on October 4, 1957, by the Soviet Union. The United States followed with *Explorer 1* on January 31, 1958. Yury Gagarin, a cosmonaut (a Russian astronaut) became the first human in space on April 12, 1961. Alan Shepard, an American astronaut, followed closely behind, traveling through space for fifteen minutes on May 5, 1961.

These exciting missions into space were watched closely by the whole world, but on July 20, 1969, the biggest space event yet was shown right on television: The crew of the *Apollo 11* landed its spaceship on the Moon's surface. Neil Armstrong and Buzz Aldrin became the first men on the Moon. The whole event was televised, and all across the world people watched nervously as Armstrong climbed out of the spaceship and stepped onto the Moon's surface. "That's one small step for a man, one giant leap for mankind," he said.

Since that first step onto the Moon, there have been hundreds of missions into space. Space stations, which are used for experiments and as bases for space exploration, have been built by the Americans and the Soviets. These allow humans to live in space for an extended period of time, conducting experiments and sending off space probes. In April 1981, the first space shuttle (a reusable spaceship) was sent on a test flight. More than a hundred successful missions have been flown in space shuttles since then.

While astronauts explore the space around Earth and the Moon, unmanned space probes have been sent all over our solar system. No astronauts have yet been to another planet, but space probes have been sent to every planet in the solar system to capture images. Sometimes they even get to land. Several probes have landed on Mars, bringing back amazing images and even samples of the Martian soil. We are learning more all the time about the other worlds in our solar system and beyond.

HAM SAYS:

FAMOUS HUMAN AMERICANS IN SPACE HISTORY

Alan Shepard	First American in space (May 5, 1961)
John Glenn	First American to orbit Earth (February 20, 1962)
Edward White	First American to walk in space (June 3, 1965)
Neil Armstrong	First man to walk on the Moon (July 20, 1969)
Sally Ride	First American woman in space (June 18, 1983)

ANIMALS IN SPACE

Before humans traveled into space, scientists ran many experiments to make sure it was safe. First, spaceships were sent up without living things inside. When those ships were proven safe, scientists began sending small animals on short space flights. The first animal to orbit Earth was Laika, a dog sent into orbit by Russian scientists in 1957. After Laika, rats, mice, rabbits, fish, frogs, honeybees, fruit flies, and even spiders were sent. The first monkey sent into space was Gordo, a squirrel monkey sent up by NASA (the National Aeronautics and Space Administration) in 1958.

HAM SAYS:

Over two thousand jellyfish have been sent into space in a NASA program designed to determine the effects of weightlessness. Jellyfish were chosen because they develop so quickly, carrying out their whole life cycle in about a year. Jumping jellies—that's a lot of jellyfish!

On January 31, 1961, Ham became the first chimpanzee in space. Ham was born in West Africa and was brought to Holloman Air Force Base in New Mexico in 1959. (He was named after the initials of his base, the **H**olloman **A**erospace **M**edical Center.) After much training, Ham went up for a 16.5-minute flight through space in a Mercury Redstone rocket. He flew up 157 miles at 5,857 miles per hour! He was also weightless for 6.6 minutes.

HAM SAYS:

On November 29, 1961, a chimpanzee named Enos was the first chimpanzee to orbit Earth. Enos was trained with a system that gave him a reward when he made a *correct* move and a punishment when he made a mistake. During the flight, the spaceship malfunctioned and punished Enos for every correct move he made. But Enos knew the right things to do and continued as he had practiced, ignoring the malfunction. See—chimps are smarter than humans!

After his return to Earth, Ham lived at the Washington Zoo for seventeen years and then moved to North Carolina.

Ham's flight made astronaut Alan Shepard's first mission into space possible four months later. Other chimpanzees in the space program continued to pave the way for human astronauts until the Air Force stopped using them to test space flights in the 1970s. In 1997, many of the chimpanzees from the flight experiments and their children were sent to a reserve for chimpanzees in Florida.